# THE ARCTIC FOX

# THE ARCTIC FOX

## MARY ELLIS

ILLUSTRATED BY
KADY MACDONALD DENTON

Collins
*An imprint of* HarperCollins*Publishers*

For Mum and Dad, with love

First published in Great Britain by Collins in 1998
Collins is an imprint of HarperCollins*Publishers* Ltd
77-85 Fulham Palace Road, Hammersmith, London, W6 8JB

1 3 5 7 9 8 6 4 2

Text copyright © Mary Ellis 1998
Illustrations copyright © Kady MacDonald Denton 1998
Cover illustration copyright © Rachael Phillips 1998

ISBN 0 00 185675 8

Printed and bound in Great Britain by
Caledonian International Book Manufacturing Ltd, Glasgow G64

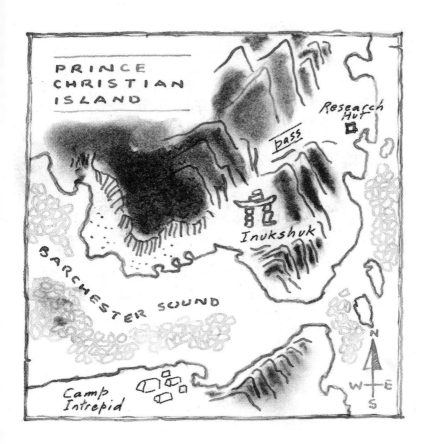

PRINCE
CHRISTIAN
ISLAND

pass

Research
Hut

Inukshuk

BARCHESTER SOUND

Camp
Intrepid

N
W E
S

# CHAPTER 1

# Dad

I used to feel it wasn't much fun being the child of an explorer. I was always the one left behind. I could only travel in my dreams and imagination.

My friends all thought I was terribly lucky to have a dad like mine. When they came to our house for tea he would sit on the kitchen table and tell us fantastic stories of his adventures. Once, he even produced the fossil of a dinosaur egg from out of his pocket. My friends didn't seem to understand that hearing his stories wasn't the same as being with him on his travels. I longed to be able to see, just once, the valleys and hills, the buried cities, the sunsets and the animals that Dad described so excitedly.

That all changed last year. You see, Dad had come home from a long trip to a jungle on the island of Sri Lanka. He had been exploring the site of a lost city. As he put down his bags in the front hall, my mother walked out on us.

In a funny sort of way it was a relief. Although Mum was the one at home, she'd always been so distant. Dad was everything to me. Now I didn't have to worry about her shouting at him any more.

"But what sort of life can I offer you Alex?" said my dad, looking bewildered and confused.

"We'll look after each other," I said.

"Yes," said my dad with a flash of inspiration, "I'll stay at home and write." Then he paused. "What about food? I'm only good at opening tins and lighting camping stoves."

"But Dad," I said, "*you're* the one who's always told me that you can do *anything* if you read enough about it."

"Even housework?" he remarked doubt-fully, looking at a huge stack of mops and dusters.

"Yes," I said firmly. "We'll read the labels on

each of the bottles and work out what to do."

We settled into a peaceful life. Dad's funny-shaped tools, microscopes and diagrams, which had always been confined to his study, crept out into every room. You may think it odd, but it became perfectly normal to find myself eating breakfast with a large piece of rock from an ancient civilization on the chair next to me.

One evening, Dad was sitting on the floor with all his maps around him. I was making a path of huge, paper dinosaur footprints leading to the back door. I opened it and looked out.

"Good heavens, is it a Brontosaurus?" laughed my dad.

There wasn't a Brontosaurus but it was snowing again. That's the best thing about living in Scotland. Large, fluffy flakes that caught in the light from the door were tumbling through the sky. Already the garden had been transformed into a land of strange, white shapes.

Forgetting my coat, I stepped outside. The flakes brushed against my face. My slippers crunched in the powdery snow. And then I saw them. *Perfectly formed little paw prints in the*

*snow.* I knew they weren't Charlie's paw prints. (He was our neighbour's cat.) Sometimes on rainy days when Charlie followed me into the kitchen he left little muddy marks on the floor. *These* prints were different.

The snow muffled my footsteps. I followed the paw prints and they led me to our old pine tree. Pushing back the branches, I peered into the clearing inside. Two gleaming black eyes gazed back at me in the darkness. I did not want to scare it away, whatever it was. I stayed as still as I could, hardly daring to breathe.

Quite suddenly, snow that had piled up on a nearby branch fell to the ground. It sent up a white spray. I jumped. There was a scrabbling sound from inside the tree. I just managed to catch a glimpse of a white fluffy tail as it disappeared through a hole in our fence.

I crouched down and waited, hoping that the creature with the shiny black eyes might return. Something glinted and caught my eye. I felt the snow, where it had been disturbed, under the hole in the fence. My fingers touched something hard and sharp. I looked closer. It was a *tooth*.

# CHAPTER 2

# The Tooth

It wasn't until I was in bed, later that night, that I showed Dad the tooth.

"My goodness, how extraordinary," he said at once, examining the tooth closely. He looked deep in thought. "Did you *really* find this outside in the snow?" He took my hand and hurried me downstairs into his study. He sat me on his huge leather chair, covered me in a tartan rug and then started to search through his books.

"Amphibians, marsupials, marine mammals.

There!" he exclaimed triumphantly as he placed a large book on my lap. It was open at a picture of an enormous whale.

"Your tooth comes from a whale, in fact it is only the very tip of a whale's tooth."

"But how can you be sure?" I asked.

"The shape," he explained, "it's unmistakable."
He showed me another book full of pictures of teeth. We looked at the tooth under a magnifying glass and then compared it with

the one in the book.

"It matches perfectly," I said.

Dad came and sat next to me. He switched on the light in his globe. It shone on the white lands at the top and bottom of the world. He began to read to me from his book, *The Frozen Land of Beyond*. Gradually his voice started to fade, until only the rhythm was left.

I didn't even notice Dad carry me to bed that night. My dreams were full of pictures of whales, cold oceans and the wind howling all around me.

When I woke up the next morning the snow was still falling outside. Dad had pinned a big piece of paper onto my favourite bear saying:

NO SCHOOL TODAY –
TOO MUCH SNOW!

I ran to the window and blew misty breath on the pane. A long icicle hung from the gutter above. I started to draw on the pane when, suddenly, I saw something dart across the garden. I opened the window and waited. Eventually, from behind the trees came a small creature. I recognized that white fluffy tail and the shining black eyes, but now I could see clearly that it was a fox. It wasn't rusty red like the ones in pictures. It was *pure white*. It had thin legs and its body was a furry pillow of whiteness. In amazement I watched as it started to play, climbing up and down over the garden fence. It stopped every now and then, ears twitching when it heard a rustle of wings in the trees, or the distant rumble of a car.

Excitement had frozen me to the spot, but seeing it playing made me wish I could get closer. I don't think I've ever got dressed so quickly. I rushed down the stairs two at a time and ran through the house. When I opened the back door the little fox didn't stop playing, even though the sound was far noisier than the rustle of trees. I stepped outside but he didn't seem scared. He didn't dart away. He just moved to a safer distance and stared at me. It was almost as if he had been waiting for me all along.

# CHAPTER 3

# Siku

The little white fox and I just looked at each other. I felt I ought to introduce myself, but words didn't seem the right way to do it. Then I remembered how much Charlie loved raisins. There were some in the kitchen.

I walked carefully towards the back door and the little white fox followed me. I stopped and so did he. I started walking again and he followed. It was like a game of grandmother's footsteps.

I opened the door and went into the kitchen.

The little fox watched me from the door. Raisins, I thought quickly. What else? The biscuit tin caught my eye.

As I came to the door, the little fox was back by the garden fence waiting for me.

"Hello," I whispered, crouching in the snow. "I'm Alex. I've brought you some food. Thank you for waiting for me." My voice was crackly and breathless. The little white fox came right over to me and ate the raisins that I dropped in front of him. I broke a biscuit. I ate half and held the other half out for him. He moved even closer and started to nibble the biscuit out of my hand. The warmth of his nose and his tongue surprised me.

"Alex!"

The sound of Dad calling my name startled the silence. The fox turned and scampered towards the gap in the fence. There was no time to think. I had to follow. I ran into the trees, wriggled through the fence and struggled to my feet. Snowflakes kept landing in my eyes, but I could still see the little fox up ahead.

I scrambled through the newly fallen snow. The little fox darted across it. He seemed to glide, hardly leaving a track. I kept slipping and sliding, panting with effort, then I took one big step and sank up to my knees.

That was it. I'd lost my friend now.

It took me ages to struggle out of the hole I had made. But as I turned the corner by the post box, the little white fox was sitting there waiting for me. He set off again. I wasn't chasing him; he was leading me somewhere. I felt sure of that.

My heart quickened as he disappeared through a large, broken part of an old stone wall. I followed and came out into a dark dell of trees. We padded between the long, snowy arms of branches. I knew I shouldn't have come this far on my own, but I had to know where the little fox was leading me.

Then a stifled cry rang through the trees.

"Here… I'm over here!"

The little fox's pace quickened and he sprang through the snow. Breathless I ran too now, and then I tripped, the biggest trip of all. Everything went white.

I brushed the snow off my face and looked

up. The little fox was crouched by the side of an elderly man who lay very still. The man's face winced with pain but lit up when he saw me.

"Well done, Siku, you found a little friend. Why, you look like a snow fox as well. You aren't, are you?"

"No," I answered cautiously.

"Blasted ankle. I tripped and fell. Can't move now – never had such a cold backside."

I crawled over to him.

"Silly of me, really," he said, "thought I was your age again. When I saw the snow, I rushed out for a run with Siku. Now look at me." The little fox licked his cheek lovingly.

"I'll get help for you," I said, finding my voice. "Dad's at home… he'll come. He could bring the sledge."

"I'd be very grateful," muttered the man.

"Good for you, Siku, finding help. I was afraid no one would take any notice of Siku or even see him. I'm Aloysius by the way, Aloysius Beardsley, and you are?"

"Alex," I said. "Here, have my coat. It might help keep you warm."

"Take Siku with you, he'll be company. I'm OK."

"I won't be long," I promised.

"Thank you, Alex." Aloysius Beardsley smiled a far-off smile. I knew he was in pain.

"Come on, Siku," I whispered, "let's follow our tracks back home."

# CHAPTER 4

# Aloysius and the Arctic

"Stay with us for a while," said my dad. "At least until it stops snowing."

"Well," said Aloysius looking pleased, "I suppose I'm already wearing your jumpers and slippers. So why not!"

Dad had brought Aloysius back and he had settled himself on our sofa. He was buried under a pile of blankets and his leg was propped up on a pile of Dad's books.

The snow continued to fall for three days. In between snoozes Aloysius talked about his travels as a wildlife cameraman.

"Then in 1968 we filmed the Komodo dragon."

"A real dragon?" I said doubtfully.

"Largest reptile in the world, Alex," said my dad. "A giant lizard. The size of this room."

"We went to Indonesia to film it," continued Aloysius. "Blasted boat that took us to the island made me seasick."

He told us of treks through the Namib desert in search of the Strand wolf and of the hours he waited in the rainforest to see a Caiman crocodile.

"What about Siku, Aloysius?" I said finally. "How did you meet him?" I had been desperate to ask him this question. Siku had become more and more friendly and he now even let me pat him on the head.

"It was only last year that I was able to fulfil

my lifelong ambition," began Aloysius. "I was asked to go to the Arctic to film polar bears. I could hardly wait. I packed my bags at once. Everyone said I was far too old. Fools! The frozen North would kill me, they said. But where do you get in life, if you don't take a chance now and then?"

Dad looked at me and smiled. He was listening too.

"It was the fifteenth of March. Spring was creeping slowly into the Arctic. I'd come far that day to a remote valley and I was very excited. The film I'd taken was of a mother bear and her babies slipping and sliding down a snowy mountain slope. They were playing and calling to each other. It was getting late by the time I got back on my Skidoo."

"Skidoo?" I asked.

"Yes, it's like a motorbike on skis," explained Aloysius.

"That sounds like fun."

"It is!"

"Suddenly I noticed that the blue sky had gone. A dark mist was rolling towards me fast. I realized that I couldn't go on. I could see nothing at all – only an eerie whiteness. A savage wind gripped me and chilled me from head to toe. I don't mind telling you I was terrified. All I could do was curl up against the Skidoo and let the snow gust against me. I had to stay awake. If I fell asleep I knew I would die.

"But it was so cold, I began to lose hope. Then, through the mist there came a small white, fluffy creature."

"Siku!" I cried. Siku's ears twitched at the mention of his name.

"Yes," said Aloysius, "dear Siku, he came over and curled up against me. He licked my cold face... but he wasn't alone. There was a dark figure with him. I tried to call out but the cold gripped my throat and my eyes blurred. I started to drift in and out of consciousness.

"Next time I woke, I was wrapped in warm skins. The little fox was still curled up against me. All the time I sensed the dark figure moving around me. Sometimes a warm liquid was spooned into my mouth. Sometimes a gentle hand touched my throat."

"To feel your pulse," I suggested. The memory of this time seemed to have turned

Aloysius' face very grey. He moved restlessly in his makeshift bed.

"The next thing I felt were strong arms carrying me. I was tied to a sledge. I drifted off again. The movement of the sledge rocked me into mysterious dreams. If my eyes opened, it was only to see a foggy whiteness and Siku trotting next to me.

"I was found by the American scientists, outside the weather station at Camp Intrepid. Siku was curled up at my feet."

"What about the dark figure?" I asked.

"There was no one else. He had disappeared. I was suffering from hypothermia and frostbite in my toes. Blasted cold. They decided to fly me back home. They knew I'd have to stay in hospital a long time."

"What about Siku?"

"He came too. He wouldn't leave my side. He howled when anyone tried to call him away. I was too sick to ask, so they assumed he must be tame and part of the documentary. They flew him back with me. While I was in hospital, Siku went into quarantine. Then, of course, I discovered his collar."

"Collar?" I repeated.

"Yes, Siku was wearing a collar made of whale's teeth."

"The whale's tooth!" exclaimed Dad in amazement.

"You've already seen the collar?" asked Aloysius in surprise.

"No," I explained, "but on the night I first saw Siku, I found a whale's tooth. It was in the snow at the bottom of the garden. We couldn't understand it."

"Come on Siku, let me show them," said Aloysius. Aloysius parted his thick fur to reveal a strange collar.

Dad fetched the whale's tooth from his desk. Aloysius held it up next to the other bones. It matched perfectly.

"The tooth must have broken off Siku's collar as he squeezed under the fence. Do you think it was the dark figure that put the collar on Siku?" I asked Aloysius.

"Yes, I'm sure of that," Aloysius paused. "Sometimes at night I dream I'm back in the Arctic and that I'm searching for him. He and

Siku saved my life. I want to thank him and to return Siku to his Arctic home. But look at me now, old and decrepit, with this blasted ankle…"

# CHAPTER 5

# Woollen Underwear

Aloysius' remarkable story reduced us to silence. The clock ticked loudly on the mantelpiece.

"The snow's stopped falling," I said absent-mindedly.

"Then my hibernation must be over," joked Aloysius. "It's time I went home."

The following day the sun came out, school re-opened and Aloysius set off. He walked with the help of an old wooden walking stick that we had found in the attic. Siku trotted at his side.

After they'd gone there was an emptiness in the house that we hadn't felt since my mum left. I was worried about Siku and how he'd manage in the hot summers. I also wanted to know more about the dark figure who had saved Aloysius' life.

A few days later I wandered into Dad's study to find him staring hopelessly at his globe.

"I don't know what's the matter with me, Alex. I can't get Aloysius' story out of my mind. I'm a fifty-year-old explorer and I live in Scotland, 500 miles from the Arctic Circle, but I've never seen the Arctic for myself."

"Well, let's go then!" I said.

"Where?"

"To the Arctic of course! We'll take Siku back and see if we can find the dark figure for Aloysius."

My dad looked stunned. "But Alex, what about school? We'd need to be gone for at least a couple of months."

"What's school compared to a trip to the *North Pole*," I said. "I've got the rest of my life to go to school. Anyway, you can teach me. You know more than anyone else in the whole world!"

Dad laughed. Then he thought. "I suppose you could go to an Inuit school while we were there," he said.

"Yes," I agreed, secretly hoping he'd forget.

"After all, I couldn't go without you," continued Dad. "But what about money? How could we pay for our trip?"

"What do you normally do?" I asked.

Dad wasn't listening, he was burrowing through his desk drawers. "Why is it that you can never find the one thing you want when you most need it?" he said, becoming agitated.

"Ah! Here we are!" He was holding a letter. *"Myths and the movement of civilizations,"* he read. *"A four-day seminar at the Royal Geographic Society, an invitation to lecture.* Well of course," said Dad, muttering to himself as he paced up and down, "ancestors of the Inuit crossed from Asia to America during the last Ice Age and they brought their myths with them. What better than to go to the Arctic to talk to their descendants and get sponsored for doing it! It'll bring the Ice Age to life."

My heart missed a beat. "Well, that settles it," I said quickly.

"I suppose it does," said my father happily. He was already studying his atlas.

Aloysius was as excited as I was about the trip.

He said he'd contact the Base manager at Camp Intrepid to arrange a cabin for us.

"Wonderful chap, Geoff," said Aloysius. "He looks as wild as an old mountain lion, but you won't find anyone as kind and intelligent. End of March will be perfect."

A day didn't go by without Aloysius phoning with suggestions and offers of essential items to include on our trip.

"A torch, waterproof matches, woollen underwear and plenty of it, Alex; climbing rope…"

Dad, as always, prepared for the journey in his own methodical way. He visited the library and took out every book he could find on the Arctic. Then he retreated to his study to read every single one.

Meanwhile, Siku's loyalties were divided between Aloysius and me. We sometimes found him sitting outside the back door in the morning. It was almost as though he understood about the trip.

"Silly, isn't it," I said, looking at the ever-growing piles of provisions, "that we need all this to survive and Siku manages perfectly well as he is."

"Which reminds me," said Aloysius one day. "When you're on the Base, Alex, it's important that you find someone there who will look after Siku when you've left. He might have become so dependent on me to feed him, that he can no longer find his own food in the wild."

"The dark figure," I promised. "That's who we'll find."

# CHAPTER 6

# Siku's Whale

I sat next to the window on the plane. There was a sea of clouds below us. I thought about Aloysius' last words…

"Start your search with the Inuit, Alex, tell them about Siku's collar."

Aloysius had come to the airport to say goodbye to us. He clutched a small, brown paper package in one hand. Siku was on the lead beside us. He rubbed up against Aloysius' legs as a big box was brought out. It was a kennel that Siku had to travel in. He would be with the luggage in the hold on the plane. Aloysius bent down to Siku, he tickled his ears and rubbed his fur.

"Here Siku, this is for you to play with on the journey." He opened the package. It was a small blue whale. Siku sniffed it. Aloysius put it in the kennel. Siku followed it into the box.

"Blasted cold, it's making my eyes water," said Aloysius. He looked so sad.

Dad wheeled the box towards the baggage handlers, when suddenly we heard a loud squeak from inside, followed by several more.

"Oh, he's found the whale's squeak." said Aloysius. "That'll keep him happy. Off you go now. Get on the plane. I promise I'll wave until you're out of sight."

As night fell we looked down on towns and cities lit up in the dark.

"Aloysius told me that in the middle of the

Arctic winter it's sometimes dark all day," I said.

"Yes," said Dad thoughtfully, "a lot of the Inuit myths started as a way of passing time in those long, freezing winters. I've just read a story about a man who kept daylight in a sealskin bag in his igloo. His daughter would play with it like a ball when he was asleep."

As we flew through the night, I felt happy that we had the light flashing at the end of the wing to lead us through the darkness.

We had to change planes in a place called Labrador. Dad and I were feeling a bit worried about Siku. We put on our warm anoraks, trousers, woolly hats and boots, then rushed off the plane to wait for his box to be brought out. Siku was quite happy, fast asleep, with the blue whale under his chin.

Our next plane, *The Polar Wind*, was small and old-fashioned. It had skis instead of wheels to land on the Arctic snow.

We watched with wonder as the city below us disappeared, then the green, and finally the trees, until all we could see was snow and great white mountains.

"Look!" cried Dad suddenly.

"There it is," said the pilot. "Camp Intrepid." In the distance we could see a huddle of buildings half-buried in the snow and lights twinkling in the darkening evening sky.

A few minutes later, the plane touched down with a startling *bump* and raced along the icy runway. A marshaller was waiting to guide us into the Base. There was a small figure next to him who was waving at us.

I'll always remember the feeling of cold as I was helped off the plane by the pilot's huge hands. The wind bit at my skin. Siku was let out of his box and he started to race round and round us, barking loudly.

"Look! Siku's happy to be home!" I shouted.

"Careful, your face will freeze," said an unfamiliar voice. A big balaclava was pulled down over my head so I could only see out of the tiny eye slits. My father's beard had gone white and frosty before he had time to pull on his hood.

Dazed by the freezing wind and the roaring of the plane's engines, Dad and I were helped onto a large snowmobile. The small figure, who turned out to be a boy a bit older than me, loaded our bags onto the back. A tall man with a booming, friendly voice drove us off the runway. It was Geoff, the Base manager whom Aloysius had told us about.

"Perfect timing, you two, the winds are picking up again tonight. Thought you wouldn't make it. Gather you've eaten on the plane..."

We drove through a cluster of snow-buried buildings.

"Well, this'll be your cabin," Geoff said as the Skidoo stopped at a small wooden hut. He unlocked the door and showed us in.

"Welcome to the Arctic!" he exclaimed as he waved his hand towards a trestle table, two old rickety beds and a big iron stove. "You light it like this. I expect you'll be wanting some shuteye so we won't be disturbing you any more. We'll see you tomorrow. Come on, Canny," he said as he put a protective arm over the boy's shoulder. Canny grinned at us and waved goodbye as they started up the snowmobile again and disappeared into the night.

"Well, now to make this new home ours!" said Dad. "That's what I always do."

After lighting the stove the way Geoff had showed us, Dad lovingly unpacked his books and notes and arranged them in the only drawer. I found Aloysius' map in my bag and pinned it to the cabin wall. I drew a picture of Dad, Siku and I and stuck them onto the map by the huts marked 'Camp Intrepid'.

"And so our mission begins," I whispered to Siku, who was curled up next to me on my bed.

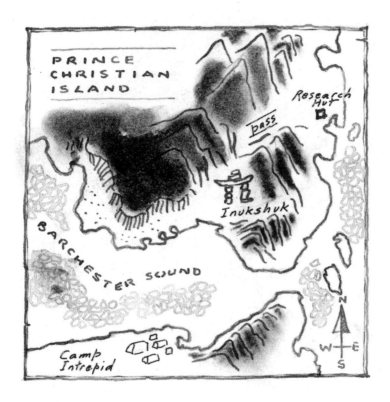

# CHAPTER 7

# Canny

The wind howled against our cabin door all that night. Siku tossed and turned at the end of my bed, but I must have got to sleep somehow because I woke to sunlight falling on us through a tiny snow-dusted window. Dad was fast asleep under a pile of books, he must have read deep into the night. I moved the books and covered him with a blanket. I scribbled him a note:

*Siku and I are off to explore.*

I shut the cabin door gently behind us. The

cold air made me catch my breath. I pulled on my balaclava. I was surprised at how many cabins there were around ours. Smoke puffed out of their chimneys into the clear, blue sky.

"One blast of wind, Siku, and those cabins look like they'd blow away." It was strange to see animal skins hanging next to the washing on the clothes line. The sea around Camp Intrepid was frozen into a vast expanse of ice.

A bell rang somewhere nearby. Siku, who'd been chasing his tail in circles, rushed off. I ran after him, round a corner and straight into a line of children standing outside a large cabin. They turned and stared at Siku and me. They all wore the same kind of furry jackets and one of them was holding onto a sledge. There was a skin bag attached to it and in it sat a girl with huge brown eyes. Her face crinkled into a tiny smile as Siku sniffed the bag. Before I could speak, a small bustling woman walked towards me.

"*Koanakotit,* Alexandra. Welcome! You've come to our school on your first day. Follow us in now."

It was a shock to discover that she knew who I was. I realized that news must travel fast here at Camp Intrepid. The last thing I wanted to do that morning was to go to school, but I was trapped. She had spoken in a tone that gave me no choice.

"Come on, Siku. We'll get it over with today," I whispered.

We joined the end of the line. As I reached the door I saw a small sign attached to the school wall:

## NO PETS ALLOWED

"But I can't leave Siku behind!" I gasped out loud. Aloysius had warned me about the Inuit hunters who trapped foxes for their fur.

A boy who had been standing nearby rushed forward and said, "Quick, put on my jacket. It's bigger than yours and you can hide your fox underneath it."

I realized that it was the boy, Canny, who'd taken us to our cabin the night before. There was no time to lose. I did as he suggested. Siku, thinking this was a new game, wriggled inside the jacket and licked my face.

"Siku. No! Keep still!" He was a heavy weight to carry. My heart was beating fast as we walked up the steps into school.

"Good morning, Canny, I hope you're going to try harder today," said the same small woman. She followed us into a tiny classroom. The children were taking off their coats.

"Shall I take yours, Alexandra?"

Before I could answer, Canny interrupted:

"Oh no, Miss Ukiup, Alex isn't used to the Arctic yet. She even feels cold indoors!"

Miss Ukiup looked concerned. "I'll turn the heating up. I've never had a child feeling cold in my school before."

"Thank you," I muttered. Siku wriggled. Canny was stifling a grin.

"Mrs Masak is away today," she continued as Siku wriggled furiously, "so I'll be taking your lessons. We learn in Inuit and English,

Alex, but today we will speak English."
Suddenly I saw Siku's white paws on my lap.

"We'll begin with…" Siku's nose appeared,
"…some maths." She turned towards the
blackboard just as Siku came right out and
dropped onto the floor. I didn't dare to look at
Canny.

"Let us estimate the width of our
classroom." Siku was sniffing around the
desks and between the chairs. The other
children began to giggle. Miss Ukiup was
about to turn round when Siku placed his
cold, wet nose against the back of her leg and
gave it a big lick.

Miss Ukiup's squeaky chalk froze on the
board. She looked down at Siku. Siku looked
up at her. There was a silence that seemed to
last for ages and then she shouted at the top of
her voice:

"Get that fox out of here!"

Siku darted out of the door.

"Quick, we'll lose him!" I cried. We dashed after Siku, past the astonished faces of the class.

"You! Come back here!" Miss Ukiup shouted after me. "How dare you bring that animal into my school."

We ran out of the school and kept on running until at last we caught up with Siku. Canny and I collapsed in the snow, helpless with laughter.

"Well done, Siku, that showed her."

Siku started to wash himself, quite unconcerned by the commotion he had caused. Canny's hands touched Siku's collar. He stopped laughing.

"Whale's teeth, Alex? Where did your little fox get this collar?"

I remembered Aloysius' words. Now that

Canny was my friend, and I knew I could trust him, I told him the story of the collar and of our mission.

"I remember," said Canny. "They found your friend by the weather station. My aunt told me about it." Canny gazed at the whale's tooth collar in silence for a few moments.

"Alex, I have a whale's tooth necklace that is *exactly the same*... My father made it for me and one for my mother. That was before he... left." He stood up quickly and grabbed my hand. "Follow me, I'll show you."

# CHAPTER 8

# The Shaman

We ran through the huts with Siku at our feet, until we came to one with a huge black bird painted on the door. Canny knocked. There was no answer.

"Sila! Sila!" he called. "He's not there," said Canny, banging on the door once more in frustration.

"Who is Sila?" I asked curiously.

"He's my grandfather, the Shaman."

"Shaman?" I repeated.

"Yes," said Canny proudly. "He's our wise

man. Don't you have Shamans in England? He is named after the spirit who brings the weather."

"Look!" I cried. Canny's last bang had unlatched the door. It swung open silently.

"Quickly," said Canny, "before we are seen." He pulled me into the hut. Siku walked ahead of us. It was as though he knew where we were going. We were in a dimly lit hallway. On a table was a candle that lit up a carved wooden figure of a man lying in a box, with a huge bird on top. Its wings were spread wide.

"See," said Canny.

"What is it?" I whispered.

"It's a Shaman getting ready for a journey. The Shaman's spirit is said to fly all over the earth, to the moon and into space. He can see everything."

I looked at Canny and shivered. "What if he

can see us now?" I asked.

"He probably can," laughed Canny. "But we'll be gone by the time he gets back."

I was quite unprepared for the room that we came to next. A strange birdcage full of candles hung from the ceiling. The candles flickered and sent creeping shadows around us. The room smelt of dusty attics and the floorboards creaked beneath us. As my eyes got used to the light, objects began to emerge from the darkness; odd-shaped plates fixed to the wall with the black bird painted on them. A fierce wooden mask made me jump with fright.

"It's a Shaman's headdress," reassured Canny, when he caught sight of my startled face. It looked like a bear's head with feathers for hair and strange carved wooden teardrop beads that fell from the mouth.

"It's in here," called Canny. He knelt down

by the side of a chest. He opened a drawer in it and carefully pulled out a little skin bag.

"Look," said Canny, "here's my whale's tooth necklace. See, it's exactly like Siku's, with the carved wooden bead between each tooth. And here Alex, look, I nearly forgot…" Canny pointed to one of the beads.

I took the necklace into the light to see it more clearly. "It's an owl," I said.

"Yes," said Canny. "It was my father's signature. You see, his name was Ranti and that means owl. He was an artist and he signed all his work this way."

"I wonder if Siku's collar is signed?"

We called Siku over and turned the collar through his soft fur. "Yes, it is!" I cried. There, on one of the beads, was an identical owl. A prickle of excitement rushed down my spine.

"Canny," I asked with renewed urgency. "Where is your father? Maybe he could tell us more."

"My father left our camp and went off into the wilderness six years ago, when I was a small boy." He paused. The smile had left his face.

"You see, my mother was drowned when their canoe hit an ice floe. My father blamed himself and in his sorrow left the camp. He told my grandfather that he had failed as a husband so he could never be a proper father." Canny's voice had gone very quiet as he explained this to me.

"Some scientists found my father's diary on a deserted island four years ago. They say that no man could have survived the harshness of these past winters. They say he must have died."

It was then that an idea suddenly came to me, something that seemed perfectly clear.

"Listen, Canny, if your father made Siku's collar perhaps he could have been the dark figure that saved Aloysius' life and brought him to the camp... and that was only a year ago, so your father could still be—"

"Alive," whispered Canny. His dark eyes gleamed with tears and excitement.

As if from nowhere a huge shadow stood

over us. A voice that was slow and powerful echoed angrily around the room, speaking words I did not understand. I stayed very still. Canny jumped up. Seemingly unafraid, but most respectful, he answered back. Siku didn't stir. As the person came closer to the light I saw his wrinkled and weather-beaten face. His old sealskin parka was covered in turquoise beads.

As Canny spoke, the old man's mouth twitched with a smile. He came over to me and clasped my hands between his. He spoke.

"Sila says you are welcome

after all," translated Canny. "He says you are not to blame for following his scoundrel of a grandson, that's me!"

I smiled and the old man laughed.

"He won't speak or learn English," explained Canny. "He believes that this is the language that has brought ruin to the Inuit people."

Sila went over to Siku and very gently looked at the whale's tooth collar. He nodded his head, stood up and beckoned Canny and me into the corner of the room. In this corner there was a huge, round basket. The lid had a handle in the shape of two polar bears. Sila handed me the lid and bent over the basket. He pulled out a carved wooden box and gave it to Canny. He led us into the centre of the room and we all sat on the rug.

Sila turned to Canny and spoke. Then, as his

words rang out, Canny translated them for me.

"Your mother came to me when you were born and asked why she had dreamed that you had to be called Cannique. As you know it means 'journey through the falling snow'. Now I know what I did not know then. Your English friend is right. These two necklaces are a sign that your father could still be alive. You must make your journey through the snow to search for him. This box contains objects that will help you. Always remember that man's spirit, when it burns with love, is more powerful than the wind and stronger than the ice."

While Canny translated his last words, the old man moved away. Eclipsed by the shadows, he disappeared into the darkness.

# CHAPTER 9

# 'Where the Ice Bears Roam'

We knelt on the floor by the wooden box.

"Look, Canny, your father's signature again," I said, pointing to an owl that had been carved on the lid. The hinges were stiff and it took both of us to force the lid open.

Small bundles that were wrapped in a yellowy material were piled inside. Canny picked one out and opened it. It contained a model of a kayak, the Inuit canoe, with oars and a tiny harpoon.

"It's beautiful," I said to Canny. He nodded

gravely, opening another bundle. This time it contained a strange ivory pipe decorated with the silhouettes of Inuit people, reindeer and two tiny carved polar bears.

"'Where the ice bears roam'," translated Canny from a tiny inscription on the side of the pipe. "This is my father's work," he said with pride. "My grandfather has shown me this pipe before. He said my mother used to play it to me when I was a baby."

A slip of paper nestled between two of the bundles. Without thinking I pulled it out. I was surprised to find that it was a letter written in English.

Prince Christian Island,
Research Centre Hut,
26 May 1987

Ranti Mudi's diary found in snow
32 km S. E. of the hut. We searched
for further traces of human life and
found none. We know of your loss
and regret that we can be of no
further assistance. Diary to be kept
here unless requested.

*Susan Sartog*

PROJECT FOR THE ARCTIC PRESERVATION & RESEARCH

"Prince Christian Island: that name, it seems so familiar." I knew I'd seen it somewhere before.

"It's an island half-a-day's journey away," explained Canny.

"Yes, but I've seen it somewhere important," I said, thinking as hard as I could. Then it dawned on me. "Canny, it's on the map Aloysius gave us. I pinned it on the wall in our hut. Let's go and see."

"But of course it would be, if it's a map of the area," Canny said.

"No, you don't understand. This is a map of Aloysius' journey. Where he went that day when the storm happened and he was found. We must look at it."

It was a shock to step back into the frozen, brilliant glare of a sunny Arctic day. The Shaman's hut had been so dark that I'd completely lost track of time.

"Siku! We forgot Siku!" I cried. We were about to set off, carrying the wooden box between us. I ran back to the hut. I'm not sure whether it was my eyes playing tricks on me, but Canny's grandfather was sitting in the corner of the room with his eyes closed. We hadn't even seen him come in again.

\* \* \* \*

*"There* you are, Alex," said my father as Canny and I burst into our cabin. Siku greeted him like a long-lost friend. Canny stood looking slightly awkward.

"Look at this," said my father enthusiastically, addressing Canny. "I was given it this morning. Isn't it wonderful? Methods of fishing haven't changed for thousands of years. Isn't it extraordinary that people have fished the same way here since the Stone Age."

"Yes," smiled Canny, his reserve falling away. "It's an ancient fish hook used for bait. I'll show you how it works."

Leaving them to talk, I looked at the map. Aloysius' journey to see the polar bears had taken him up the coast and onto Prince Christian Island. And there, beyond the mountain pass, was the spot where the mist and storm came. This was too much of a coincidence.

"Canny, look!" I called him over to the map. "Look, it *was* Prince Christian Island where Aloysius ran into the storm."

"...and the scientists' hut is *there*," said Canny, pointing to a square drawn on the map. "So thirty-two kilometres south-east would be about *here*. That's where the diary was found." Canny and I gazed at the map in excitement.

"We'll look in the diary," I added. "It might help us."

"Am I allowed to know what's going on?" said my father, amused. "It sounds like you two already have an expedition planned."

Together, Canny and I poured out the story of what happened in Sila's hut.

"You must talk to him, Dad, he'll be able to help you with your lecture." We showed Dad the box and the letter from Prince Christian Island. He agreed that the coincidences were remarkable.

"So we must go, mustn't we?" I said.

"Yes, yes, I suppose we must," agreed Dad. "But I've got to admit that I'm a bit worried about leaving the Base so soon. After all, I've only just unpacked and hardly put my nose over the doorstep. Then there's the matter of Skidoos and equipment. Geoff—"

"There's nothing to fear," interrupted Canny. "I've been on many expeditions with my uncle. He and Sila have told me all there is to know about survival in the Arctic. It's in my blood," he added proudly.

"So we'll be fine," I said.

"Well, I suppose we will," said Dad, but I saw a troubled look on his face.

"We are true friends now," said Canny. "For in Inuit we have a word, *Angoniakat*, which means we trust a person enough to go on a journey with them." Canny rubbed Siku's ears affectionately. "I am staying with my aunt and uncle. You must all come there and eat with us. Yes, you as well, Siku. They will be pleased to meet you, everyone is talking about you! It's muklak fish for lunch, an Inuit speciality, they brought it back from their last fishing trip."

"Where do you live, Canny?" I asked.

"Sometimes with my aunt and uncle, other times with Sila or if a plane is arriving at the Base, Geoff and the team let me stay with them."

As we were walking with Canny to his aunt's cabin, a flock of barnacle geese flew overhead.

"Look, Alex, a sign of hope!" Canny shouted as the cold wind tossed his words into the sky.

# CHAPTER 10

# Prince Christian Island

"Minus thirty-eight degrees centigrade," exclaimed my dad. "It's the coldest day we've had yet." We were finally ready to go. Fierce storms had kept us at Camp Intrepid for three days. With the winds blowing outside and Canny's aunt and uncle cooking us delicious meals, we had watched as blizzards rearranged the Arctic scenery.

These three days gave us a chance to get used to our Arctic home and I was able to ask Dad about the worried look on his face.

"It's Canny, really," said Dad. "I'm afraid that all these strange coincidences are raising his hopes falsely. He seems happy in his life on the Base, now his spirits could be dashed forever."

"Remember what Aloysius said," I argued. "Where do you get in life if you don't take a chance? If we don't help Canny search for his father he'll be left wondering forever. Anyway," I finished, "I don't believe Sila would send us on the journey if he didn't think that there was real hope."

My father smiled at last. "Spoken like a true Inuit, Alex. You'll have to help me give my lecture when we get back."

Dad and Sila had got on immediately. They'd spent hours talking together. Canny was their often-weary translator.

When Sila went back to his cabin for a rest, Dad wrote up his notes. Canny, his uncle and I, packed and repacked the sledges.

"Now then," I said, "food for six days, candles, matches, first-aid kit, socks, flares in case of emergencies."

Siku's new game was to climb all over the sledges just as we were fastening down the tarpaulin. He seemed to sense the excitement of the days to come.

Canny's aunt and uncle lent us two Skidoos to draw the sledges. Canny and I were to take it in turns to drive one and my father would drive the other.

We made Siku a little seat on Dad's sledge. We sewed Aloysius' squeaky whale onto the seat so that Siku would have his companion with him. He chewed it happily.

We were masked against the icy wind and dressed in real caribou skins that Canny's aunt had insisted on us having.

"They're warmer than any anoraks you can buy," promised Canny as he inspected us proudly.

Just as we had started our engines Sila appeared. He was shouting at Canny.

"What's he saying?" I asked. I was sitting behind Canny on the Skidoo.

"He's asking us if we remembered to take some musk ox wool."

"Why musk ox wool?"

"To fish," said Canny, laughing. "He's an old worrier really. He says, 'teach them to fish the Inuit way, save supplies and remember the lessons I have taught you'."

Sila stopped shouting, shook my father's hand, patted me on the shoulder, gave Canny a hug and stood back to wave us off.

We had worked out that it would be a day's journey to the hut on Prince Christian Island. We had to travel along the coast. As we whizzed smoothly along, the freezing wind bit against any parts of my skin it could find and took my breath away. I looked back, but already Camp Intrepid had disappeared, lost in the blizzard of snow thrown up by our Skidoos. Now we were on our own.

We looked to our left and saw dark gleaming mountains with deep valleys between them and to our right we found ourselves passing a strange-looking world of shapes, where the sea ice had frozen into castles and dragons.

"Dragons – where?" said Canny, overhearing me thinking aloud. He brought the Skidoo to a halt and so did Dad. We stared in amazement at the strange landscape.

"Look over there," said Canny, "baby seals! It's a sign that spring is here. We must be quick otherwise the ice will start to melt and we won't be able to cross to the island."

It was my turn to drive the Skidoo. Sometimes a mirage lifted the pack ice into the sky. At times Siku would grow restless with chewing his whale and he would jump down and chase after us instead. His blue shadow scampered beside him in the bright sun. Across the sea ice I now saw great mountains, their snowy tips turning pink in the evening light.

"*There*! Look! It's Prince Christian Island," yelled Canny. "We must cross the ice *right now!*"

I hadn't realized how bumpy and uncomfortable the crossing would be.

Strangest of all was the thundering sound that our Skidoos made on the ice, as though the sea beneath was full of roaring monsters.

I could now see the southern end of the island more clearly. The jagged drifts of snow and ice were so steep that we had to push the Skidoos. It was exhausting and my legs began to ache.

"The cabin!" called Dad suddenly. He was pointing to a hut that stood like a welcoming beacon in the distance.

I suppose I'd imagined it would be cosy and warm inside. Instead, it was like the Snow Queen's palace. Tables, chairs and the bunks were covered in frost. Icicles hung from pots on the ceiling.

"It's freezing, even colder than outside," gasped Dad.

"Fire," said Canny, "that's what we need. I saw driftwood on the shoreline that we can use to light the stove. Alex, you find the musk ox wool. We can have fish for supper."

We collected driftwood and soon it was crackling and hissing in the stove and turning our frozen fairy-tale world into a steamy kitchen.

Then Canny showed us how to fish like the Inuit. "Now dangle the line through the holes. By jigging it about, the fish is tempted to swim closer and then you spear it. The Inuit learned to fish this way by watching polar bears."

Canny and Dad decided that I'd make a good polar bear, because I caught two Arctic char fish and they didn't catch anything.

While we were sitting at the long trestle table waiting for the fish to cook, Canny and I looked at each other.

"The diary," I said. "Let's look now."

# CHAPTER 11

# The Diary

"The scientists told us to look for the diary in an old chest underneath the wooden bunk beds," remembered Dad. "And I've got the key they gave me in my rucksack."

"Here's the chest," said Canny. "But the lock's frozen."

"Pass me a candle," I suggested. "We'll try and warm it." After holding the candle under the lock for a minute or two, the key turned stiffly.

We searched through a pile of books, maps

and other objects. Each one was labelled carefully, like exhibits in a museum.

"My father's name. Look! On this label," exclaimed Canny as he picked a small leather-bound book out of the box.

"Don't sit in the dark, bring it over here under the lamp," said Dad.

Canny turned the pages of the book and I realized that he was trembling slightly. Most pages were headed in faint spidery writing.

"The date," explained Canny. "It's the same as the year it was found." Below this there were pencil drawings. Some pages had tide marks as if the book had got wet and dried out again, and some were even torn, but all of the drawings looked beautiful to me. There were polar bears, seals, owls, every polar creature you could imagine.

"But nothing at all that helps," said Canny, thinking aloud.

"No clues at all," I said, disappointed. My father was examining the diary with his magnifying glass.

"Canny, what does this say?" On the last page there was some writing. Some of it was illegible.

"Crack—" said Canny. "Then something I can't read… that's strange."

"What?"

"Well, it says 'moon'."

"Crack, moon," repeated my Dad.

"A crack in the moon? It doesn't make much sense," said Canny.

"How about an eclipse?" I cried.

"But that's when the moon is completely dark," said Dad.

"I'm sure it's important," said Canny. "The moon plays a very special part in our folk tales. My grandfather has often told me stories about Tarqeq, the moon spirit. But a *crack*, I can't think of a story about that. Still, it's a start," said Canny, undeterred by this setback.

We agreed that the next day we would press on to the spot where Aloysius had his accident in the storm. I was still longing to see a polar bear.

Later that night, as the embers from our fire began to die, I woke up shivering with cold. I got up to find an extra jumper. Then I saw that Siku was awake, too. He was sniffing earnestly at the diary. Every now and then he made a strange whimpering sound. I tiptoed over to Canny and shook him. We tried not to wake Dad.

"Look at Siku, Canny, look." Canny's eyes took a while to focus. "He recognizes something," I said. "The scent…"

"Of someone he knows," whispered Canny in amazement. "My people would say that Siku is giving us a sign to persevere."

The following morning the weather had changed from the brilliant, clear day on which we had set off. It was cloudy and the island seemed dark and forbidding. We were heading south-west, up towards the mountain pass that would lead us to the other side of the island. The compass was fixed to the Skidoo. Canny had the binoculars to scout out the pathway ahead.

"Look out for shadowy areas of ice," shouted Canny.

Ice meant that the Skidoo would lose its grip or, worse than that, it could plunge into a deep and hidden hole. The higher we got, the more difficult it became to see. The slight breeze turned into a wind that grew stronger and stronger. Soon the wind was blowing so strongly that we couldn't see a thing.

"You can't tell the sky from the snow," said Canny from behind me. "We'll have to walk."

I stepped off the Skidoo and slipped – there was no warning. The snow gave way beneath my feet and I fell. Somehow Canny grabbed me and heaved me backwards, calling for my dad to help. Together they pulled me to safety.

As though in a nightmare, we saw a great crevasse open up beside us.

"Biscuits, where are those chocolate biscuits?" asked Dad urgently. We looked at each other. Canny pointed to the bag on the sledge.

"Take them, Canny. Throw them out, one by one, in front of the Skidoo. If they disappear, we'll know there's a crevasse ahead."

Slowly we moved on. Sometimes a biscuit disappeared and we had to make a wide detour. It seemed forever that we had to inch our way forward.

"The Inukshuk! We've made it!" cried Canny. "Look, Alex!" He was pointing to a huge pile of stones that suddenly loomed ahead of us through the mist.

"It's the marker. I remember it on the map at the end of the pass."

"A sentinel rock!" cried my father in relief. "Who wants the last chocolate biscuit?" At this remark Siku pricked up his ears and came over to Dad. He nibbled at the biscuit.

Canny and I had been amazed by Dad's quick thinking back on the pass.

"It's simple," he said. "I read somewhere about Inuit trackers who used the same technique with frozen reindeer droppings."

"Well," I laughed, "there can't be many people who can honestly say that their lives were saved by a packet of chocolate biscuits!"

# CHAPTER 12

# Wolves, Polar Bears and Gulls

By the time we crossed the pass, darkness was falling and the visibility was so bad that we decided to pitch our tent by the sentinel rock. The sides flapped wildly in the wind as we struggled to put it up. When it was finally done we crawled, exhausted, into our sleeping bags.

"Have you got my extra jumper? Alex, those are *my* socks," grumbled Dad. "How's an explorer suppose to keep his feet warm these days? And have you both done your teeth?"

"But our toothbrushes are underneath your

pillow," said Canny.

"We won't bother then," said Dad wearily.

Siku couldn't make up his mind where he was going to sleep and kept climbing over us. He chewed our toes and licked our ears affectionately as he made up his mind.

"Siku, you're making us dizzy," laughed Canny. "Settle down."

Suddenly, Siku's ears pricked up and Canny's laughter faded. There was a terrible howling outside that made my flesh creep.

"It sounds like wolves," said Dad anxiously.

"*Wolves*," I whispered. Canny was listening intently.

"It *is* wolves," he said, "but it's nothing. Just one pack warning another not to come into their territory." All the same, I noticed Canny huddle closer to my dad in his sleeping bag.

\* \* \*

The third day of our journey dawned. The storm had passed over us in the night and it was another beautiful clear morning. I felt a tremendous sense of disappointment. Had I imagined that the dark figure would come to us in the storm like he did to Aloysius? I suppose so.

Canny must have thought the same thing. He just looked at me and said, "Promise we won't talk about it being our last day before turning back."

"I promise," I said with feeling.

From our spot by the 'Inukshuk' stones, the snow-blown mountain slope led down to the seashore. It was called 'Barchester Sound', on Aloysius' map. The frozen seashore stretched into the distance until it came to cliffs that towered high above it.

"Quick! Dad, where are those binoculars?" I

called out.

"What have you seen?" he asked, handing them to me.

"Bears!" cried Canny, pointing to the foot of the cliff. We watched as two polar bears lumbered across the ice and dived into deep green pools of icy water.

"Hunting for seals," said Canny. The water swallowed them up. We watched transfixed until suddenly one of the bears broke the surface to breathe.

"We're safe now!" yelled Canny. I'll race you to the shore!" and he set off sliding down the slope. I tumbled after him.

The cliffs high above us were lined with thousands of guillemot birds. The chicks were trying to reach the sea, but many of them would crash-land on the shore.

"Stop, Siku!" I yelled. "Look, Canny, he's heading for the baby gulls." We ran down to the seashore shouting at Siku who looked like he'd decided to have one for his lunch.

"Canny, I'll distract Siku! You help the gulls to reach the water."

At one point I managed to throw a snowball so far that it hit the cliffs. Siku headed after it and I ran laughing after him. Tears froze to my cheeks. The next moment I found myself gazing at the foot of the cliffs. Siku had disappeared inside a cave, but it was the entrance that stopped me dead in my tracks. It was a huge crack, shaped like a crescent.

"It's shaped like the moon," I said to myself.

"THE MOON," I yelled. The words caught in the wind. "CANNY!" I cried, "A CRACK… I'VE FOUND IT… A CRACK IN THE SHAPE OF THE MOON!"

# CHAPTER 13

# The Cave of the Moon

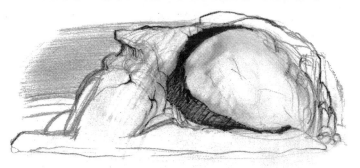

Canny hadn't heard me. He was carrying one of the baby gulls down to the water.

"Canny, quick! You must come."

Canny gazed up at the entrance to the cave. "So that's what those words in the diary meant; a crack in *the shape of* the moon. I wonder if Siku knew it was here all along?"

We lit the candles and entered. Inside was a huge and hollow cavern. We ran all over it, searching for signs of life.

"Nothing," said Canny after a few minutes.

"No skeletons, even," he said, trying to laugh.

"No treasure," I muttered, thinking of *Treasure Island*.

"Look at Siku, Alex. He's found a ledge to sleep on. It could have been made for him," said Canny. He sat down. I gazed helplessly round the cave and back at Siku.

*It could have been made for him.* Canny's words flashed through my mind. I rushed over to the shelf.

"Look Canny, it *has* been carved." At the same moment we saw the little owl that was set in the stone by Siku's paw. A shiver ran down my spine.

"Your father's signature."

"So you see, it really *must* be my father's cave," Canny said to my dad. We'd brought him inside and shown him the signature on the ledge. Just to be sure, we had compared the owl signature in the cave to the one on the wooden box.

"… and look at the crack," I added. "It's just like the diary says." Now we were both convinced that Canny's father was the dark figure who had saved Aloysius' life.

"But of course," said my dad. "Why didn't I think of it before? Rock caves are the obvious place to live and shelter in the Arctic wilderness." He moved off with his torch to look deeper into the cave.

Dad suggested we bring the sledges and Skidoos down to the cave and spend the night there. A mist was rolling in and the jewel-like ice pools looked dark and menacing. We were so busy talking and unpacking that we took a while to notice that Dad had disappeared. We shouted for him. There was no reply. After a delay that felt like a lifetime, Dad's voice called out:

"Over here, I've found some bones."

Canny and I looked at each other in alarm. We rushed around a niche at the back of the cave to find Dad holding up a bone in the light of his torch.

"What kind of bones?" I asked nervously.

"I'll have to check my books, but I'm convinced that they once belonged to a woolly mammoth and must be a million years old! Take a look, you two. Quite remarkable; the most exciting find I've ever made." Canny and I examined the bones with immense relief.

That night, as we ate our supper in the cave, Canny was full of optimism. "Now that we've found my father's cave, I know he can't be far away."

My dad was preoccupied with his mammoth bones, but I was worried. Why, I thought to myself, would the cave be so empty if Canny's father was still alive? Maybe it *was* him who saved Aloysius' life, but that was a whole year ago and there had been a harsh winter in between. Could we be too late?

I couldn't bear to say any of this to Canny. If only Sila had been nearby to talk to.

Perhaps Dad was right after all. Maybe all

we'd done was give Canny false hope.

# CHAPTER 14

# Footsteps

After the candles had burnt low and Dad had fallen asleep, a curious sound echoed through the cave.

"Canny, did you hear that?" I whispered.

"Mmm… yes," said Canny sleepily, "it was footsteps – I think."

"What if it's a polar bear?" I trembled. Our candle flickered and went out. A dark shadow crouched at the entrance to the cave. My hand was on a loose rock. Dad was fast asleep, snoring gently.

"I'll throw this into the air," I thought, "that will scare it away." From beside us Siku rushed to the shadow. It raised its arms and turned.

Siku jumped up at it and started barking. I heard my father stirring in his sleeping bag. The next moment the beam of his torch lit up the face... of a man. The man was patting Siku and speaking softly to him. Canny climbed slowly out of his sleeping bag and stood up.

The man gazed at him, startled. Canny spoke in Inuit and the man stared at him in amazement. Then he turned and hurried out of the cave. Siku followed him. Dad and I rushed to the entrance of the cave just in time to hold Canny back. He was ready to run after the man into a thick and blinding mist.

"Canny," my dad spoke forcefully now, "remember that in a mist like this you can be completely lost in seconds. You could be only a few steps from another person and yet never see or hear them. What good would that do?"

"But I'm sure it's my father!" cried Canny in despair. "What if he doesn't come back? Why didn't he speak?"

Then I noticed the wooden box containing Canny's father's work.

"Look at the box, Canny," I said in amazement. "It's *open*." We had left it next to the sledges at the mouth of the cave. We began to search through the contents.

"The pipe's missing," said Canny in excitement. His whole body was trembling now. "It *must* be my father. Who else would bother with it?"

Canny and I decided to sit at the entrance to the cave in our sleeping bags and wait for the mist to lift. We must have fallen asleep because we awoke with a start to my dad shaking us gently.

"Alex, Canny, it's morning! Don't worry," he said, seeing our anxious faces, "I've already been outside and spotted something around the headland. We haven't explored that far yet. Come with me."

"Look," he cried as we rounded the headland. There, on the sunlit shore, was an igloo and outside it lay Siku, curled up and fast asleep.

As we got closer to the igloo we could hear the music of a pipe being played from inside. It was a beautiful sound. Canny walked to the entrance of the igloo and called out his father's name. "Ranti!"

Siku stirred and looked round into the igloo. A few seconds later a man emerged.

He was quite small and dressed in skins that were sewn roughly together. He had a dark, weather-beaten face and the blackest eyes I'd ever seen. Like Sila, you felt his presence from a distance. He stared at Dad and me and then at Canny. Finally, Canny managed to say *Appak*, the Inuit word for father. After a pause, the man said something in angry tones and before we knew it, he had gone back into the igloo.

Canny didn't speak, he set off down the shore. I ran after him and found that he was crying. "Canny, what did he say? Is it really your father? Please tell me."

"Of course it's my father," sobbed Canny. "He hates me. We must leave here today!"

"But Canny," I persisted. "What did he say to you?"

Tears ran down Canny's face as he repeated his father's words. "I see your mother in your face."

My dad was thoughtful when I told him this. "Canny," he said firmly, "do you remember what Sila said about saving supplies and fishing the Inuit way? If we do that we can stay here for at least one more day. We must give your father a chance to get to know you. Some people need more time than others. It's more of a shock for him to see you, than for you to see him. He has lived alone for all these years."

"But do you think he'll ever speak to me? Do you think he'll come back with us?" asked Canny desperately.

"I don't know," said my dad. "He's been on his own for a very long time."

We were all busy that morning with fishing and cooking on the seashore. Canny's father sat outside his igloo, watching us. There was a moment when Dad had problems lighting the fire in the blustery wind. Ranti came over to him. He took the flame, showed Dad what to do and then returned to the igloo.

I could see the look of sadness on Canny's face at the presence of his father so close to him.

Later I had an idea. "Canny, does your father speak English?"

"Yes," said Canny. "He went to university in Vancouver. He studied English and Art."

I picked up the box of Ranti's work and walked across the snow to him. I laid all the contents out at his feet.

"Your work?" I asked.

He looked at me and then down at the objects. Very slowly he picked up the kayak and turned it over in his bare hands.

"Yes," he answered. Suddenly he pulled out the tiny oars and the kayak separated into two pieces, revealing a secret compartment. Inside was a scroll of paper. Ranti unfolded it. He looked at it and turned away. I picked up the paper, and saw a drawing of an Inuit baby. Underneath it was written 'Cannique'.

I rushed back to Canny with the drawing. "Look, this must be a sign that he cares for you."

"In that case why won't he talk to me?" sobbed Canny.

I took Canny off to play snowballs with Siku, but his heart wasn't in the game. He just kept looking over towards his father. We watched as my dad went over and sat by Ranti. He told us that he had talked to him about his travels around the world, and about the thrill of finding relics such as the mammoth bones, until finally Ranti started to talk to him about Inuit origins and myths.

Canny became increasingly hurt by all this.

"He can talk to both of you but not to me."

"That's because you mean so much to him," explained my dad. "I think Ranti doesn't know how to treat you because you were just an infant when he left. Sometimes I'm still amazed that Alex isn't a baby any more."

Canny said nothing. He didn't need to. We could feel his tremendous sadness. He was so different from the lively boy we'd first met at Camp Intrepid.

# CHAPTER 15

# Lost Links

That evening was the mildest yet. We could tell that spring had come.

"Too warm," muttered Canny as we sat out by a fire on the shore. We were lost in our separate thoughts so it was a shock to look up and see Ranti coming towards us. He sat down, slightly outside the circle of firelight. My father passed him some food and he ate it in silence.

Siku was sitting close to me. His warm body gave me the courage to ask the question that I'd longed to know the answer to.

"Please tell us about the whale's tooth necklace. Why does Siku wear it?"

"There were two whale's teeth," began Ranti. He spoke in a low murmur, with a strange rhythm to his words. His voice had a singing quality, like the wind. "Sila, my father, gave them to me. He'd been given them by his grandfather. I carved two necklaces out of them. One was for my son, Cannique, and one was for his mother. The whale has the greatest spirit of all and it was to protect them both, the two people I loved most..." He paused. His body shuddered. "The necklace was left behind on that day we went hunting. Later, when I left the camp alone, I took it with me. Now 'Siku', as you have called him, wears it..."

"What did *you* call him?" interrupted my father.

"*Makkuktut.*"

"Nuisance," translated Canny.

"Yes," and Ranti laughed, for the first time. It was a loud hearty laugh, but he still did not look at Canny. "Nuisance, because each time I tried to fish, I'd cut my hole in the ice and he'd splash in the water, or he'd bark, scaring off the fish."

"Then why did you put the collar on him?" I asked.

"Because he was my constant companion and he accepted me as I was. He seemed to want me as a friend. I gave him the collar to protect him."

"And that's how it all began!" I exclaimed. Ranti looked questioningly at me. So I told him about finding the tooth in the snow, then seeing Siku and him leading me to Aloysius.

"A determined old man," smiled Ranti. "It was Siku that found him. We were coming back to the cave from the north side of the island, across the pass. There was a terrible storm and Siku found him lying in the snow. I built him an igloo and warmed him with some reindeer milk I had with me. He grumbled a lot."

"I bet he did," laughed Dad.

"He went in and out of consciousness,"

continued Ranti. "For two days I nursed him, but I realized he needed to see a doctor. I was used to storms, they were my friends, they made me invisible. I put the old man onto my sledge and dragged him back to Camp Intrepid. I left him there, by the weather station, where I knew he'd be found within a few minutes. I left. I couldn't be seen. I've given up that old life."

"What about Siku," I said. "Why didn't he go back with you?"

"He had found someone who needed help more than me. He stayed curled up next to the old man to keep him warm. Who was I to call him away?"

The next few seconds, after he had finished speaking, seemed interminable. Dad broke the silence, saying:

"You know we must go back tomorrow."

"Yes," said Ranti, "the ice will be melting. For your own sake you must not leave it any longer. You have delayed long enough."

"Will you be coming with us?" asked Dad, gently. Ranti stood up abruptly and walked hurriedly back to his igloo. Siku scampered after him. It was as though he had dismissed us.

"Father! Father!" cried out Canny. He ran to the edge of the circle of light and sank to his knees. "He speaks as though I'm not here. I understand now, he wishes I was dead, too – I've lost him and now Siku's gone as well."

Dad and I stood next to him, helpless in the face of his sorrow. The fire burnt low as Canny stared towards the dark shore.

# CHAPTER 17

# Pack Ice

All that was left of Ranti's presence in the morning were scattered blocks of broken igloo on a bleak and frozen shore. I had hoped that Siku would stay with us, but he was gone too.

Dad and I packed the sledges. Canny just sat by the cave. He couldn't even bring himself to help.

"Come on, little cob," said my father tenderly. "We're ready to go."

It was a clear day, so the shadowy patches of ice were easy to spot as we travelled back over

the pass. It was hard to imagine the troubles
we'd had on the way over. But at least we had
hope then, now there was none.

It was early afternoon when we eventually
reached the south shore of the island. We were
just about to set off across the ice when Canny
tensed from behind me on the Skidoo and
shouted:

"Stop! Don't go!" Fear had woken him from
his preoccupations. "It's too warm. Look! The
ice isn't safe, it's *cracking*!"

Sure enough, we felt the ice heave beneath us and we watched a patch break away to reveal icy green sea. Dad and I were alarmed.

"We'll have to go back to the scientists' hut," said Canny. "We'll wait for help. The Base will be alerted when we don't return today."

I was gazing out across the sea ice. There, in the distance, was a figure hurrying towards us.

"Look, Canny, someone's coming! They must have known we'd be in trouble."

As the figure drew closer, Canny, who was standing beside me, rushed forward. "*Father*, it's my *father*!" he cried out.

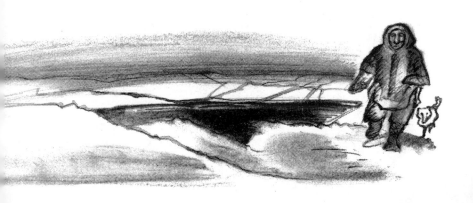

Dad and I looked at each other in panic. Could Canny just be wishing it was Ranti? Then, to our joy, we saw Siku. It really was Canny's father. Siku scampered in circles round us, but Ranti spoke urgently.

"You'll need to go across the land path. It is still safe. I know the route. Follow me."

Canny was shocked. "You're coming with us?" he asked.

Ranti put out his hand to Canny and for the first time looked straight into his eyes as he spoke:

"I realize that you are alone and so am I. What is the sense in this? I would like to be your father again."

Canny hesitated and then he ran towards his father and put his arms around him. They hugged as though the years had never separated them. The shadows of their loneliness seemed to melt away.

Together, with Siku at their side, they set off across the ice that would lead us to safety and to the warmth of Camp Intrepid.

# POSTSCRIPT

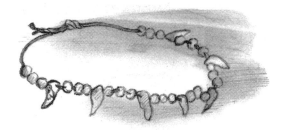

"My blasted luck I missed all that!" said Aloysius.

We were still sitting on our luggage. We'd just got back and Aloysius had met us at the airport.

"Canny wanted you to have this; it's his whale's tooth collar. He says it's all thanks to you and your determination to film the polar bears that he and his father found each other."

"Nonsense," scoffed Aloysius, looking proudly at the collar. "It was Siku, of course."

"What do you mean?" I said.

"Well, I reckon he knew Canny's father was ready to return to the real world. He set off with me to bring him back. The Inuit believe that all Arctic creatures have a soul."

"Do you know, Sila said the same thing," I exclaimed. And then, for one very clear moment, I thought I could see Siku scampering ahead of me just as he did that first day when we'd rescued Aloysius.

"He made all our dreams come true, in the end," I whispered to myself.